Sidewalk Trip

Patricia Hubbell pictures by **Mari Takabayashi**

HarperFestival®
A Division of HarperCollinsPublishers

I'm dancing down the sidewalk
with a hop, hop, hop.
Pigeons peck at popcorn
with a *pop, pop, pop.*

Doggy wags his tail
with a *woof, whiff, woof.*
Pigeons fly away
to a big red roof.

I'm splashing through a puddle
with a *splish, splish, splish.*
Ice cream! Ice cream! Ice cream!
is my wish, wish, wish.

Bicycles are racing by—
their wheels all go *whizz*.
I think I hear the ice cream truck—
I know just where it is!

I'm jumping down the sidewalk
with a leap, leap, leap.
Baby in a carriage
is asleep, sleep, sleep.

Kids are running past me
with a skip, jump, yell.
I bet they hear the ice cream man's
tinkle, tinkle bell.

I'm marching down the sidewalk
on my own two feet.
Policeman at the corner
whistles *tweet! tweet! tweet!*

I take my Mama by the hand,
we cross the busy street.
Ice cream in a cone
is our drippy, drippy treat!

Traffic light is changing
with a *flick, flick, flick.*
I'm eating up my ice cream
with a *lick, lick, lick.*